In the spirit of celebrating
diversity, a portion of the
proceeds from the

Brookie Cookie Bookie

will be donated to
organizations that assist
children and families facing
a wide variety of adversity.

BROOKIE COOKIE BOOKIE

A children's book about friendship, acceptance and celebrating our differences

Written by Robin B. Rosenberg

Illustrated by family and friends of Brookie Cookie

My name is Brookie Cookie
And I'm three years old
My favorite color is blue
And I don't like being cold!

I have lots of friends
We like different toys
But we all play together
And find common joys.

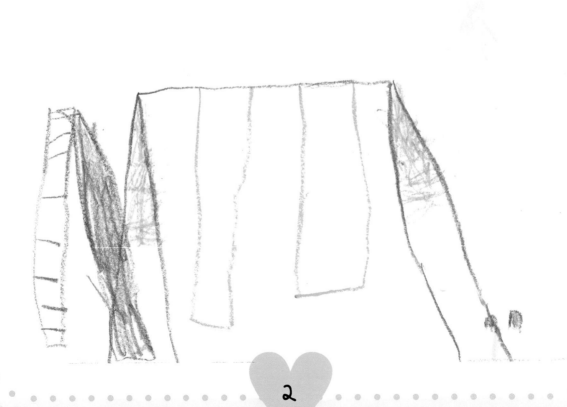

2

I love the beach
And Reese loves the pool
But we both love to swim
And eat ice pops to stay cool!

I play soccer
And Jaden likes karate
But we both love exercise
And moving our body!

I love wearing bracelets
And Macy prefers rings
But we both love jewelry
With lots of sparkly bling!

I am really loud
And Sophia's really shy
But we both love the park
And a big ole pizza pie!

My hair is curly
And Gigi's hair is straight
But we both love pigtails
And think lollipops are great!

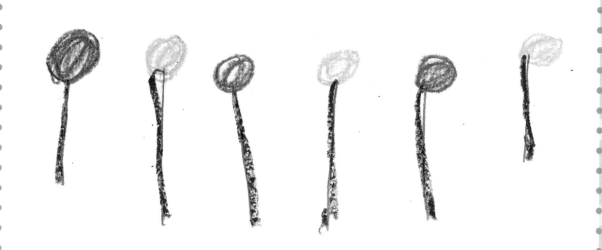

I love to sing
And Molly loves to dance
But we both love music
And my neighbor's doggie "Lance!"

Lance

I celebrate Hanukkah
And Maddy celebrates Christmas
But we both love presents
And butterfly kisses!

9

Tess loves tea parties
And I'd rather read
But we both love the library
And making necklaces with beads!

Annie loves the summer
And I love fall
But we both love winter
And making humongous snowballs!

I love ballerinas
And Emily prefers princesses
But we both love dress up
And talking about our five senses!

I drink water
And Aidan loves juice
But we both love chocolate milk
And reading Dr. Seuss!

Kate loves bananas
And I love grapes
But we both love watermelon
And sure do love to bake!

14

I love trucks
And Shane loves boats
But we both love to paint
And tell funny jokes!

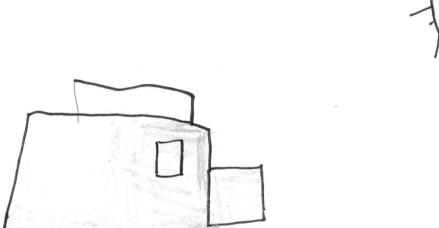

15

I love ice cream
And kyra loves cake
But we both love dessert
And jumping in lakes!

16

Samara has red hair
And mine's light brown
But we both love to giggle
And wear a princess crown!

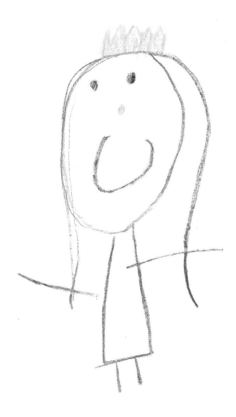

Siobhan has a BIG family
And mine's very small
But we both love family time
And know it's the most important
time of all!

Mommy   Brookie   Daddy

Anna loves butterflies
And I prefer ladybugs
But we both love
Grandma and Grandpa
And their great big giant hugs!

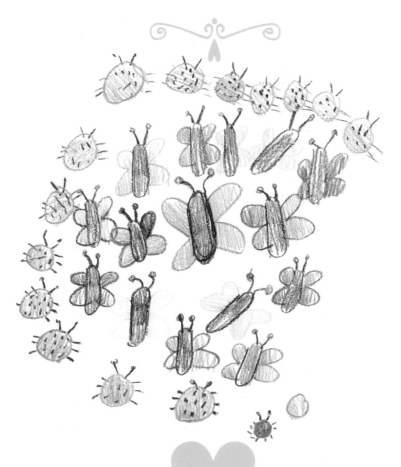

I love to run
And Livy loves to climb
But we both love balloons
And reading nursery rhymes!

Gavin loves to surf
And I like biking
But we both love Mother Nature
And always recycling!

Please
Recycle

21

Gabi loves to read
And I love art
But we both love friends & family
With all of our heart!

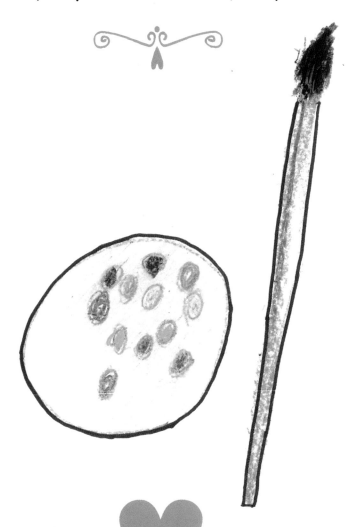

22

Loud, quiet
Short or tall
No matter our differences
Love unites us all!

23

The aspiring little artists
listed below have created the
illustrations you've enjoyed in the
Brookie Cookie Bookie.
I hope they have inspired other
little artists everywhere.

Jaden C.

Macy C.

Reese C.

Gabrielle H.

Gavin H.

Sophia I.

Ciara L.

Ryan L.

Brooke R.